A Special Place for Edward James

SHIRLEY ISHERWOOD

A Special Place for Edward James

Illustrated by David McKee

HUTCHINSON
London Melbourne Auckland Johannesburg

First published in 1988 by Hutchinson Children's Books
An imprint of Century Hutchinson Ltd
Brookmount House, 62–65 Chandos Place, Covent Garden
London WC2N 4NW

Century Hutchinson Australia Pty Ltd
16–22 Church Street, Hawthorn, Melbourne, Victoria 3122

Century Hutchinson New Zealand Limited
32–34 View Road, PO Box 40-086, Glenfield, Auckland 10

Century Hutchinson South Africa (Pty) Ltd
PO Box 337, Bergvlei 2012, South Africa

Set in Baskerville by BookEns, Saffron Walden, Essex

Printed and bound in Great Britain by
Anchor Brendon Ltd, Tiptree, Essex

British Library Cataloguing in Publication Data

Isherwood, Shirley
A special place for Edward James.
I. Title   II. McKee, David
823′.914[J]   PZ7

ISBN 0-09-172000-1

Contents

To Oliver Leigh Caplan

A Special Place for Edward James

Edward James wanted a special place of his own. First, he tried to make a special place for himself in the attic. But the attic was full of dusty boxes and parcels. The sun only shone in for a little time each day. It was a gloomy place, and no one wants a special place that is gloomy.

Next, he tried to make a special place in the shed. But a big spider lived in the shed. It had woven a beautiful web for its own special place; and no matter how hard he tried not to be, Edward James was a little afraid of spiders.

Florence tried to make him a special place; a tent made from old curtains. But the tent always fell down, and always when Edward James was inside it.

Mr Manders saw all this, and felt a little sad. He remembered when he was a small bear, and had a special place of his own; a little wooden house, built in a tree. It had been a wonderful place. When he sat in it, he could see the sun shining in through the gaps in the roof, and he could hear the sound of singing birds, as they flew to and fro among the branches. When the wind blew, it made a sound in the tree like the sound of the sea.

Every small bear should have a tree house, thought Mr Manders, and he decided that he would make one for Edward James. He would make it that night, so that when Edward James got up the next morning there it would be, with its shining window and its door with a round brass door knob. 'And I'll make him a sign for the door,' said Mr Manders to himself. 'A sign with his full name: Edward James Fortescue.'

That night, as soon as Edward James was asleep, Mr Manders brought the wood from the shed and began to saw up the planks to make the tree house. The noise of the saw sounded very loud in the still night air – *zit-zat zit-zat.* Mr Manders felt sure that it would wake Edward James, and he crept back into the house to see if he was still asleep.

Edward James had hardly stirred beneath his patchwork quilt. He was lying flat on his back, and he was fast asleep. Mr Manders went back to the garden, and began to saw his wood again. The noise woke Florence, and she came hurrying down the path in her dressing gown. 'What on earth are you doing, Mr Manders?' she asked.

'I'm making a tree house for Edward James,' said Mr Manders. 'It's going to be very special, with a window and a door with a brass door knob, and his full name on a sign: Edward James Fortescue.'

To Mr Manders's surprise, Florence thought that this was a good idea. 'All small bears should have a tree house,' she said, firmly. 'I shall make him some cushions and some curtains.' She trotted back down the path, and soon all the lights in the summer house came on. Mr Manders heard the sound of the sewing machine, whirring away.

Mr Manders climbed the tree, and began to haul up the planks of wood on a piece of rope. The branches of the tree creaked loudly. I'm sure that Edward James has woken up, thought Mr Manders. He climbed down from the tree, ran into the house, and peeped into Edward James's bedroom. Edward James had turned on to his side, but he was still fast asleep.

Mr Manders went back to the garden. He was beginning to feel rather tired, and he sat for a moment on a branch. As he sat he watched the long grass of the field stir, as small night animals ran to and fro. He felt that it would be very pleasant to sit there until the sun came up; but then he thought of how pleased Edward James would be when he saw his tree house, with its shining window and its door with the brass door knob, and the sign that said, 'Edward James Fortescue'.

He began to nail the walls and the floor of the tree house together. *Bang! Bang! Bang!* went the hammer. From the summer house there still came the loud whirr of the sewing machine.

All these noises *must* have woken Edward James, thought Mr Manders, and he climbed down from the tree and hurried to Edward James's bedroom. Edward James was lying on his tummy with his bottom in the air, and he was still fast asleep.

Mr Manders went back to the garden, and began to climb the tree again. When he reached the first branch he sat down, and thought about how beautiful the house would be, with its shining window and its door with the brass door knob, and the sign that said, 'Edward James Fortescue'. Thinking of this, he fell asleep, and dreamt that the house was finished, and that they were all having a party inside; himself, and Florence, and Edward James, and three pink pigs. . . .

Three pink pigs . . .? thought Mr Manders, and he awoke with a start. Someone was making a loud knocking noise in the tree. Mr Manders looked up, and there was Florence sitting on the half-finished roof of the tree house. She was holding the hammer and nailing the last of the planks together. The finished cushions and curtains lay at the bottom of the tree, in a neat little pile.

'Did you enjoy your nap, Mr Manders?' asked Florence.

'I wasn't asleep,' said Mr Manders, 'I was just thinking with my eyes closed.' He climbed the tree, and put the window in its place. Then he hung the door with the brass door knob on its hinges. Florence brought up the curtains and the

cushions, and the tree house was finished. 'And now for the sign on the door!' said Mr Manders.

But when he looked for a piece of wood to make the sign, he found that there was scarcely any left. Only one small piece lay in the grass; and that was far too small to paint on it the name, Edward James Fortescue.

Mr Manders made the sign, and nailed it to the door with the last nail. *Bang!* The noise woke Edward James, and he tumbled out of bed, and ran out into the garden.

It was early morning. The sun had just risen, and the birds were waking up. Over the dewy grass ran Edward James, until he came upon Mr Manders and Florence, asleep under the tree. High above his head was the little wooden house. Edward James climbed up, turned the brass door knob, and went inside.

He sat down on a cushion and smiled. He could see the sun shining in through the gaps in the roof, and he could hear the birds singing as they flew among the branches. A little wind arose, and made a sound in the tree like the sound of the sea. Edward James watched his curtains flapping at the window. It was a wonderful house, he thought. But what he liked best of all, was the little sign on the door that just said, 'E. J.'s Place'.

The Sneeze

One morning, in the garden, Mr Manders gave a sudden, and a very loud sneeze. Florence heard him, and at once she came from the summer house, and looked at him keenly. 'Mr Manders,' she said, 'you have got a cold in the head!'

'Not really,' said Mr Manders. But even as he spoke he felt the beginnings of another sneeze, and he trotted back along the garden path as quickly as he could, and went into the kitchen. '*Atishooo!*'

The sound of the sneeze rang in his head, but his thoughts were surprisingly clear. 'One,' he said to himself, 'if a bear sneezes others are bound to think that he has a cold. Two, when they think you have a cold, they are almost bound to want to look after you – especially Florence.'

'I haven't got a cold, Edward James,' he said, 'I feel quite all right.' But even as he said this, he saw Florence come hurrying along the garden path, with a large basket and a big woolly shawl over her arm.

Mr Manders sighed. He had grown very fond of Florence, ever since she had come to live in his summer house. She was a small, tidy animal, who mostly kept herself to herself. Sometimes whole days went by without Mr Manders or Edward James catching sight of her. It was the ideal way for neighbours to be, thought Mr Manders; each living their own lives, but each knowing that the other was always there, and that if they were ever sad or lonely there was a friendly face close by.

But, like many small animals, Florence could be surprisingly bossy. (Once, she had spring-cleaned Mr Manders's house, and rearranged all his furniture.) And now she was clearly on her way to look after him.

'Say, "Thank you very much but I feel all right!" ' said Edward James.

'But that seems so ungrateful when some one is being kind,' said Mr Manders. 'Perhaps I'll let her look after me just until lunch time.'

He sat down in his armchair with a sigh, as

Florence trotted into the kitchen. Without a word, she wrapped him in the big woollen shawl and fastened it across his chest with a large safety pin. Then, from the basket, she took a bottle labelled 'Cold Cure', a dozen large white handkerchiefs, a thermometer, a hot-water bottle, her crotchet work, and a thick book, entitled *Hints For The Careful Nurse*.

At the sight of all these things, Edward James said loudly, '*I* feel all right!' and he scampered out into the garden as quickly as he could. Mr Manders watched him go. He tried to wave goodbye, but his arms were too tightly bound to his sides by the shawl. He tried to say, 'Have a nice time,' but Florence popped the thermometer into his mouth.

When she had taken his temperature, Florence placed a small pillow behind his head, a footstool beneath his paws, and gave him the warm hot-water bottle to hold. Then she sat down in the rocking chair, took up her crotchet work, and smiled happily.

For the rest of the morning, Mr Manders sat and gazed through the window, and watched the red kite flying over the field. It swooped and soared and tossed in the wind, and Mr Manders thought about how Edward James would be enjoying himself, dashing this way and that over the springy grass. Mr Manders wished that he

could be with him; but when he tried to work his trapped arms free from the shawl Florence wrapped him up again, more tightly than ever. Then she gave him two teaspoonfuls of the cold cure. It tasted surprisingly pleasant, but made him feel drowsy. Soon he was fast asleep.

When he awoke it was lunch time. Florence was busy by the stove, making a pan of soup, and Edward James was standing by Mr Manders's side, holding the big red kite. 'Have you been looked after enough now?' he asked.

'I think so,' said Mr Manders, and he got to his feet, still wrapped in the shawl.

But Florence saw him, and said, 'Sit down, Mr Manders!' in a rather stern voice.

Mr Manders sat down, and Florence smiled at him. 'One must be firm with one's patient,' she said. 'It says so in my book.' She set about rearranging the pillow and the shawl, and then she turned to Edward James. 'It also says that a cold is easily caught!' she said.

But Edward James just said, '*I'm* all right,' ate his soup quickly, and ran outside into the garden once more.

Mr Manders didn't even try to wave goodbye. For the rest of the afternoon he gazed through the window towards the field, where glimpses of the white sail of the boat could be seen, as Edward James skimmed over the pond. Mr Manders wished that he could be with him, feeling the wind on his face, and hearing the lap of the water against the sides of the boat.

Florence sat close by in the rocking chair. She sang softly as she did her crotchet work, and sometimes she told Mr Manders stories about her great-aunt Tomkins, who seemed to have had a very long and rather dull life.

Mr Manders wished that he was like Edward James and could say, 'I feel all right,' and throw off the warm shawl and trot down the garden path, without a backward glance. But when someone is being kind, and showing how very much they care for you, thought Mr Manders, it is hard to refuse their kindness and caring; it is almost as if they had given you a present and you had looked at it, and said, 'Thank you very much, but I don't want it!' Anyway, between the warmth of the shawl and the long dull stories, he was beginning to feel very drowsy again. He closed his eyes and was soon fast asleep.

When he awoke it was almost tea time, and outside the sky was beginning to grow dark. There was no one in the kitchen, but the door stood open, and there was the delightful smell of the smoke from a wood fire. Mr Manders got to his feet and, trailing the shawl behind him, went to the window and looked out. There, at the bottom of the garden, were Florence and Edward James, dancing round a bonfire made from old, dried leaves and branches. It snapped and crackled, and red and yellow sparks flew up into the air. The sight filled Mr Manders with a feeling of great excitement, for he dearly loved a bonfire. Throwing off the woolly shawl, he trotted down the garden path. 'Florence,' he said, 'I feel quite all right!'

To his surprise, Florence merely smiled and said, 'I'm glad to hear it, Mr Manders. My book says that the patient often makes a quick recovery with careful nursing!'

After the bonfire had died down, everyone

went back to the kitchen and had toast and jam for tea. Mr Manders began to look forward to all the things that he and Edward James could do in the evening. But, as soon as tea was finished, Florence sent him straight up to bed. 'It says in my book that an early night is very beneficial after a cold in the head,' she said, in a firm voice.

Slowly, Mr Manders climbed the stairs. He stood by his bedroom window, and gazed down to the bottom of the garden where faint wisps of smoke still drifted from the bonfire. As he gazed, he saw Florence go down the path with the basket and shawl over her arm. Into the summer house she went, and a moment later lit her lamp. Mr Manders could see her through her window, as she put away the things in the basket, folded the shawl, and hung the basket back on its hook. And as he watched her, he smiled to think of how carefully she had nursed him. She was indeed a kind and caring friend.

And what better present could anyone give you, he thought, as he climbed into bed, than their time, and all their love.

The Gypsy's Warning

One morning, Mr Manders heard a knocking on the front door. Opening it, he found a large brown rabbit, dressed in gypsy clothes, with a basket over her arm in which lay some sprigs of white heather. 'Buy a bit of lucky white heather, sir!' she said.

Mr Manders looked into her gentle face and great, dark eyes. It must be wonderful to be a gypsy, he thought, to sit at night by your camp fire, and to trundle off in your caravan the next morning, to who knew where.

He bought a sprig of lucky white heather, and stuck it in to the buttonhole of his jacket. The gypsy rabbit gazed at him, and twitched her nose. 'Tell your fortune, sir?' she said. 'You have a lucky face!'

Mr Manders held out his paw, and the gypsy rabbit took it into her own, and gazed at it for some time. Then she said, softly, 'Ah, but there's a little bear that loves you, sir!'

That will be Edward James, thought Mr Manders, and although he already knew, deep inside him, that Edward James loved him, it gave him a nice warm feeling to be told so.

'There's more, sir!' said the gypsy rabbit. 'There's a small, fluffy someone – I don't know quite *what* she is – but she thinks very highly of you.'

Could that be Florence, thought Mr Manders, and could it be possible that she thought very highly of him? The warm feeling grew until he felt as warm as toast. 'Thank you!' he said, and he was about to take his paw away, but the gypsy rabbit held it fast. 'Beware of water, sir!' she said. Then she turned and scurried off down the path, her red skirt and yellow shawl fluttering as she went.

'What do you mean?' cried Mr Manders. He hurried after her, but by the time he reached the end of the garden, the gypsy rabbit had gone through the gap in the fence, and was bobbing over the field. Mr Manders stood and gazed after her. At the end of the field she stopped and looked back. 'Beware of water!' he heard her call, 'Oh, heed the gypsy's warning!' And then she was gone.

Mr Manders turned and slowly made his way back to the house. When he reached the kitchen, he sat for some time at the table, with his chin in his paw. 'Beware of water!' he said to himself. Could the gypsy rabbit have meant the pond? Had his boat somehow sprung a leak, without him knowing anything at all about it? He hurried to the field and looked at the boat, which was drawn up by the side of the pond. But there wasn't the smallest hole to be seen.

Mr Manders began to make his way back over the field. As he went, he was struck by a dreadful thought: he was going to take a sea voyage! That was, without a doubt, the meaning of the gypsy's warning. He would have to make a journey over the sea, which would mean saying goodbye to Edward James, and Florence; to his house, his garden, his field, his pond, and his boat; to all the things that he loved most in the world.

The warm feeling of being loved had completely left him, and in its place was a sad, cold little feeling, which grew stronger and stronger as he made his way slowly back over the field. He felt that he must be the saddest bear in the whole, wide world. As he went he imagined how he would tie up a few belongings in a red handkerchief; for no one can take a great many things on a long sea voyage, he told himself, just some spare socks and perhaps a picture of Edward James as a momento.

The thought of going off with these few pitiful belongings brought a lump to his throat. He tried to cheer himself up by thinking of how wonderful it would be when he returned, with many a stirring tale to tell of his adventures on the high seas.

And then, an even more dreadful thought struck him. Suppose he was shipwrecked? That is what will happen! thought Mr Manders. He saw himself swimming away from the wreck to a small and quite empty island, where he would build a hut, and live alone for many years.

He would collect a pile of driftwood on the beach, and at last a ship would sail into sight, and he would light his fire. The smoke would be seen by the captain of the ship, and Mr Manders would be rescued. Home he would come in his tattered jacket, still carrying the red handkerchief, with the spare socks, and the picture of Edward James.

What a wonderful moment it would be, thought Mr Manders, standing by the gap in the fence. And then another dreadful thought came into his head: suppose that Edward James had forgotten him? If I stay away for years on the desert island, thought Mr Manders, he will be a grown bear by the time I get back. And he pictured himself walking slowly up the garden path, a bent old bear with his shabby bundle.

'Edward James!' he would say in a quavering voice, and Edward James would look at him in a puzzled way.

'Don't you know me?' Mr Manders would cry.

'Ah, yes,' Edward James would say, 'I do seem to dimly remember you.'

I will be the saddest bear in the whole, wide world, thought Mr Manders. A tear came to his eye, and he brushed it away and went in search of the little bear. He found him some time later, walking round the field.

'Edward James,' said Mr Manders, 'If I go away, perhaps for a long time, and get shipwrecked and live on a desert island, you *will* remember me, won't you?'

'Where are you going?' asked Edward James. 'And *why*?'

'I don't really know,' said Mr Manders. 'I only know I must go on a sea voyage. It was the gypsy's warning, you see: beware of water! I must have one last look at my begonia beds!' he cried. Then he ran through the gap in the fence, blinded by tears, and fell full length in the stream.

'The gypsy's warning: beware of water!' said

Edward James, trying hard not to laugh.

Mr Manders got slowly to his feet and climbed out of the stream. As he stood, dripping water on the grass, Florence came running from the summer house, carrying a big, white towel. With chattering teeth, Mr Manders told her what had happened.

'Florence,' he said, some time later, when he sat before his fire with a warm drink in his paw and his fur gently steaming, 'I don't suppose you think highly of a foolish bear?'

'Mr Manders,' said Florence, 'sometimes I think very highly of you. But not when you go on imaginary sea voyages, and shipwreck yourself—

a pair of socks in a red handkerchief, indeed!'

And despite himself, Mr Manders had to smile; for he had Edward James, and his friend Florence; he had his house, his garden, his field, his pond and his boat. He was, he told himself, the happiest, and the luckiest bear in the whole wide world.

The Explorers

One morning, Mr Manders decided that what he most wanted to do was to go exploring. 'It's the most exciting thing in the world!' he told Edward James. 'Off you go with a song in your heart and your pack on your back.'

'Where do you go?' asked Edward James.

'That is the exciting thing,' said Mr Manders. 'One never knows until one gets there. That is what exploring is: finding a place where no other bear has been before.'

Edward James thought that he would like to go to a place where he *had* been before; but Mr Manders just said, 'Nonsense!' and made a large packet of sandwiches, and a Thermos flask of tea. Then he took a stout rope from the shed, and a good thick walking stick from the umbrella stand in the hall. 'One never knows when one will need these things when one is out exploring,' he said.

'Is exploring dangerous?' asked Edward James, looking at the rope and the walking stick.

'Sometimes,' said Mr Manders. 'That is one of the best things about exploring: going into new places and saying, "Pooh!" to all the dangers that might be lurking there!'

At this, Edward James felt even less like going exploring; but Mr Manders set off briskly over the garden, so there was nothing that Edward James could do but follow him. As he went, he practised saying, 'Pooh!' softly to himself.

But it is all very well, saying, 'Pooh!' to a bear that you know, and in a place that you know. Edward James said 'Pooh!' to Mr Manders all the way across the field and down the lane, but when they reached the wood he stopped saying it and held tight to Mr Manders's hand.

'Take a deep breath, Edward James,' said Mr Manders, 'and in we go!'

So Edward James took a deep breath, and followed Mr Manders into the wood. It was a very deep and dark wood, and the further in they went, the darker it became. As he went, Edward James looked back at the sunny lane; but soon there was nothing to be seen but trees. They stood all round, with their great roots lying tangled across the path. And after a few more steps the path could no longer be seen. Edward James turned to make his way home, but Mr Manders caught him by the arm and held him firmly. 'This is what explorers *do*,' he said. 'They find a way through the wood for other bears to follow. That is what we shall do. We shall make a new path, and it will be known as 'Manders's Way''.'

'In fact,' he said, sitting down with his back against a tree trunk, 'the whole wood will be known as "Manders's Wood".' He said 'Manders's Way', and, 'Manders's Wood', several times to himself, and then he went to sleep.

Edward James sat by Mr Manders's side, and wondered why it wouldn't be called 'Mr Manders's and Edward James's Wood' and 'Mr Manders's and Edward James's Way', since he and Mr Manders had gone exploring together. He was just about to wake Mr Manders to ask him this question, when he heard a loud rustling from a large bush.

Edward James jumped to his feet, and Mr Manders awoke with a start. There, sticking out of the bush, was a long orange tail.

'What sort of animal has a long orange tail?' said Edward James.

'A tiger!' said Mr Manders. 'A tiger has a long

orange tail!' And with that, he climbed the tree as quickly as he could, with Edward James close behind him. When they reached the top they looked down. The tail had vanished, but from the other side of the bush there could be seen, through the leaves, part of an orange face, with yellow eyes and white whiskers.

'It is a very *large* tiger,' said Mr Manders. 'Since its tail was on one side of the bush, and its face is on the other, its body must fill the space in between.'

'What do explorers do when they see a tiger?' asked Edward James.

'They capture it,' said Mr Manders, after a long pause. 'They capture it and take it home with them, to prove that they have been exploring, and have been very brave.'

'How do they capture the tiger?' asked Edward James.

'With a net,' said Mr Manders. 'But I'm sorry to say that we haven't brought a net with us, so we can't capture the tiger.'

'What do explorers do if they haven't got a net?' asked Edward James.

'They wait until help comes,' said Mr Manders. 'And if it doesn't come soon, they shout for it.' And he put his two paws round his mouth, and shouted as loudly as he could, 'Help! Help! There's a tiger in the bush!'

Edward James shouted, 'Pooh!' and hoped that the tiger would go away.

But the tiger stayed in the bush. He stayed there until it was time for tea. Mr Manders and Edward James began to feel very hungry, but the packet of sandwiches and the Thermos flask were at the bottom of the tree.

'Suppose you go down, very quickly, and get them, and quickly come back up again?' said Edward James.

'Suppose I stay here,' said Mr Manders, who had no wish to be eaten by a tiger. From the top of the tree, he and Edward James could see over the wood to the field, where Florence was making her way to the summer house. They could see their own house, and the garden with the little stream. The sight made them feel very homesick.

'That is one of the things about being an explorer,' said Mr Manders. 'Sometimes they long for their home, but are very far away from it. Sometimes they sing about it.' And he began to sing, in a deep, doleful voice, 'Home . . . home . . . home, sweet, home. Where ever you may wander, there's no place like home!'

As he sang this mournful song, with his eyes closed tight, Edward James looked down at the bush, and saw a large ginger cat come strolling out. He sat down between the tree and the bush, and began to wash.

'Mr Manders,' said Edward James, 'it's not a large tiger – it's a cat.'

Mr Manders opened his eyes, and looked; then, slowly, he began to climb back down the tree, with Edward James following him. 'You see, Edward James,' he said, as they went, 'things seem much bigger than they really are, when you can only see bits of them.

'The thing is,' he said, when they reached the bottom of the tree, and stood looking at the cat, 'when you can only see bits of a thing you don't know how big the spaces are *between* the bits.'

He was getting very confused, and he felt rather foolish; so foolish that he almost wished that there *had* been a tiger in the bush. In the end he stopped making excuses, and said, 'It was just a cat who moved from one end of the bush to the other.'

They left the cat still washing by the tree, and began to make their way home. And the nearer they came to home, the better and braver they felt. 'After all,' said Mr Manders, 'for a time we thought that it *was* a tiger, and that's as good – or as bad – as if there really had been a tiger.'

Florence was sitting by the door of the summer house, as they made their way through the garden.

'We've been exploring!' said Edward James. 'We saw a ginger cat in a bush!'

'Indeed,' said Florence. But she didn't seem very interested or excited by this news; and neither Mr Manders nor Edward James felt like explaining how they had thought that it had been a tiger.

'But that's the thing about exploring,' said Mr Manders, as they went into the kitchen, 'it's much better *doing* it than just talking about it.'

The Cake

It was almost Edward James's birthday, and Mr Manders decided that he would make a birthday cake. He told Edward James to play in the field until he was called; then he got out his mixing bowl, his wooden spoon, his cake tin, the butter, flour, eggs and sugar. He also took from the cupboard currants, cherries and nuts. 'It will be the best birthday cake ever baked!' said Mr Manders.

Mr Manders made very good cakes; but a birthday cake must have icing, and the words 'Happy Birthday' written on it; and Mr Manders had never iced a cake. He put on his jacket, and hurried down the path to the summer house.

Florence very kindly told him how to ice a cake. It seemed very easy to do. Then she gave him her little icing bag. 'Fill it with icing,' she said, 'then squeeze the bag gently, and when the icing comes out at the end, write the words "Happy Birthday Edward James".'

This did not sound quite as easy as just icing the top of the cake. 'Perhaps I'd better come and help you,' said Florence, 'in case you have a little accident.'

But Mr Manders wanted to make the cake all by himself, and he hurried back to his kitchen. 'I don't see why a bear shouldn't be able to write a few words on a cake!' he said to himself as he went.

When the cake had been baked and cooled on the rack, he poured on the white icing and smoothed it carefully with the blade of a knife. It looked beautiful, like snow and ice. Mr Manders was very pleased. Then he mixed some pink icing, and began to squeeze the bag to write the words 'Happy birthday'.

But he squeezed too soon. The icing came out of the end of the bag and fell, not on the cake, but on the top of the table where it wrote a word that looked like 'Wuggle'.

Mr Manders looked at the strange word, then he hurriedly wiped it away with his paw; for he could see Florence making her way to the kitchen.

'I just came to see if everything was all right,'

she said. 'It's very easy to have an accident when icing a cake for the first time.'

But Mr Manders just waved his sticky paw in the air, and said carelessly, 'No accidents – no accidents at all! Icing a cake is quite easy!'

'Indeed!' said Florence, and she began to make her way back down the path. As soon as she had gone, Mr Manders picked up the icing bag and leant over the cake, to write the words 'Happy Birthday Edward James'. He felt a little flustered, for he could still see Florence from his window, and she looked as though she might come back at any moment. Very gently, he squeezed the bag, and he had just written the letter 'H' when Florence opened the kitchen door again. 'Are you *sure* that everything is all right, Mr Manders?' she said.

Mr Manders was so startled that he gave the bag a hard squeeze. All the icing shot out, and lay on the top of the cake like a tangled ball of pink string. Mr Manders stood in front of the cake, so that Florence couldn't see it. 'No accidents at all!' he said.

Florence gave him a close look, as if she knew that he wasn't telling the truth, then she turned and trotted back up the path to the summer house. Mr Manders looked at the tangle of pink icing, then he took his knife and patted it and poked it, until it looked like a large pink rose. Mr

Manders was very pleased. 'And now for the words!' he said.

But the bag was empty. Mr Manders mixed some more icing, and then found that he had no more pink colouring left. So he made some blue icing instead. He put it into the bag, and he was just about to write the word 'Happy' when he saw Florence coming up the path once more.

Mr Manders put his paws behind his back. He was very careful not to squeeze the bag, but he could hear the icing dripping on to the cake. 'No accidents?' asked Florence.

'None at all!' said Mr Manders.

When Florence had gone, Mr Manders looked at the cake and found that the icing had made a row of little blue balls. He flattened them gently with his paw, so that they looked like a row of little blue flowers. I can't wait to write the words, he thought.

But it was time for lunch, so he made two sandwiches and took them out to Edward James in the field.

'Why have my sandwiches got blue smudges on them?' asked Edward James.

'It was an accident,' said Mr Manders, and he hurried back to the kitchen to finish the cake.

Holding his breath and gently squeezing the bag, he began to write. But it was very difficult to do; like trying to write with a long, blue, wriggling worm. Mr Manders wrote 'Hippy'. He wrote 'Hoppy'. And, at last, he wrote 'Happy Birthday Edward James'. Then he put the cake in the cupboard, so that neither Florence nor Edward James could see it until it was time for the birthday tea.

The next day was Edward James's birthday. Mr Manders felt very proud as he carried in the cake, with all its candles alight.

'A hippy, hoppy, happy birthday?' said Florence. But Edward James didn't care at all that 'Hippy' and 'Hoppy' were written on his cake. And, indeed, it was the kind of birthday when everyone felt so happy that they cheered, 'Hip-hip hooray'; and felt so giddy and silly that they hopped about.

At last, when Edward James had fallen asleep, Mr Manders and Florence went for a walk round the garden. 'The cake was very pretty with its rose and its forget-me-nots,' said Florence. 'How did you manage to do that, Mr Manders?'

'Well, to tell the truth,' said Mr Manders, a little bashfully, 'it was an accident – a sort of happy accident.'

The Island

It was summer. Every day the sun shone from morning till night, and it was too hot to do anything at all but lie in the shade of the tree. This is all very well, when you are a large, sleepy bear; but when you are a small, wide-awake bear, it is very boring. Edward James tugged at Mr Manders's ears to wake him up, and said, 'Let's paddle in the stream!' But the stream was just a trickle of water, threading its way between the stones and pebbles.

He said, 'Let's go up in the balloon!' But Mr Manders thought it was too hot to go ballooning.

He said, 'Let's go for a walk in the field. But Florence said that he would get too hot if he went for a walk in the field. She, too, sat in the shade of the tree, and had tied up her fur in bunches, with ribbon bows, so that she would feel cooler. All day she sat and talked about her relations; of whom she had a great many.

At last, Mr Manders gave up trying to go to sleep. He took Edward James by the paw, and walked slowly with him over the field. There, to his great surprise, he found that a mysterious little island had appeared in the middle of the pond.

'Where has it come from?' asked Edward James.

'It was there all the time, under the water,' said Mr Manders. 'Now the sun has dried up some of the pond, and here is the island for all to see!'

As he stood and gazed, a wonderful idea came into his head. If the sun went on shining and drying up the water of the pond, the island would get bigger; and if it got big enough he would sail across the pond in his boat, and stay on the island until the weather grew cooler. How peaceful it would be, he thought: no more stories about Florence's relations, no more tugging at my ears! 'It will be my very own place,' he told himself. 'Every bear should have his own quiet place.'

Early next morning, just as dawn was breaking, he crept from the house and ran across the field to the pond. The island was still there. At first it looked just like a black hump in the light of the rising sun. But when the sun was fully risen, Mr Manders could see that the island had grown. One more day, he thought, and I shall be able to go.

For the rest of the day he sat beneath the tree and thought about the island. Florence told him a very long story about her great-aunt Tomkins, but he hardly heard a word. Edward James tugged at his ears, but he scarcely noticed. His mind was full of the mysterious island.

The next day, he got up very early and wrote a short note, which he pushed beneath the door of the summer house. 'Dear Florence,' it said, 'I am going to the island. I will stay there until the weather is cooler. Please look after Edward James.'

He ran across the field, pushed the boat on to the pond, jumped in and drifted slowly over the water to the island. Then he stepped ashore, and gave a great sigh of happiness. 'My very own place!' he said, 'with no one to disturb my summer thoughts.' He sat down and tried to think of a name; for it seemed important that the island should have a name. Should he call it 'The Quiet Place', or maybe 'The Peaceful Place'? Or, should it have a name like 'The Island On The Pond'? Thinking of these names, he fell asleep.

When he awoke the sun was overhead, and he was very hot. But no trees grew on the island. Mr

Manders walked all over it, but he didn't find one growing thing. It was a little bleak and barren place – and still quite muddy in parts. At last he crept into the boat, and lay in the shadow of the sail.

As he lay on the bottom of the boat, he heard Florence and Edward James calling to him from the edge of the pond. He raised his head a little, and saw them shading their eyes with their paws as they looked towards the island. Mr Manders ducked his head down again. What is the use of having your own peaceful place, he thought, if it is too hot to walk once you are there. He felt a little foolish, and stayed in the boat until tea time came and the day grew cooler.

Then he stood on the edge of the island and looked towards his garden, where Edward James and Florence went to and fro between the summer house and the tree. They're having a picnic tea! thought Mr Manders; a picnic with treacle tart! (For the delightful smell had reached him even on the island.) A picnic without *me*!

He felt rather hungry, as he had only brought a few sandwiches with him, and these had dried in the heat of the sun. For a time he sat and ate his dry sandwiches, and tried again to think of a name for his island. 'The Secret Isle'? he mused. 'The Summer Isle'? 'Bear Island'? But none of these names seemed quite right; and he had just given up trying to think of a name for the time being when he saw the lights come on in the tree – dozens of the little fairy lights that he used at Christmas. And soon after that, he heard the sound of Edward James's gramophone, playing 'Waltzing Matilda'.

Now they're having a party! he thought. A party without *me*.

He felt very sad, looking at the lights and listening to the music which drifted faintly over the field. And suddenly the right name for the island came into his head: 'The Lonely Place'.

He crept into the boat, lay down, and went to sleep. In the morning, as soon as it was light, he sailed back to the field.

Edward James was very pleased to see him. 'I want to go to the island, too!' he said. But Mr Manders just shook his head, and went to sit in the shade of the tree. Florence came and sat beside him and told him a long story about her great-uncle Albert. Edward James tugged at his ears, but Mr Manders didn't mind; he was very glad to be back in his garden.

When evening fell, he took Edward James over the field, and together they looked at the island on the pond. Mr Manders thought of the lonely time he had spent there. 'A bear needs other bears,' he said, 'and a Florence, and a garden.'

But Edward James still wanted to visit the island. 'It's a place that should just be looked at,' said Mr Manders firmly, and they turned and made their way back to the house.

In the night, it rained heavily, and when Mr Manders and Edward James went out to the pond the next morning, the island had completely disappeared.

The Visitors

One morning, Mr Manders was very pleased to get a letter from his friend, Wilkins. 'Bickers and I will come for a short stay with you on the twenty-ninth,' it said. It was written in a big, bold hand, and Mr Manders propped it by the marmalade jar, and gazed at it all through breakfast. After breakfast, he put the letter in his jacket pocket, and went for a walk round the field, with Edward James.

'How pleasant it is to see old friends!' he said, as they walked. 'In they come and you say, "Why, you haven't changed a bit!" and they say, "Neither have you!" '

'And then,' he said, settling himself beneath the hedge, 'you tell them all your news: all about your new arrangements in the garden, about your boat, and about going up in the balloon.'

He closed his eyes, and was almost asleep when he remembered that tomorrow was the twenty-ninth. At once, he jumped to his feet and together, he and Edward James hurried back to the house, to clean the spare bedroom ready for the visitors.

'Tell me again what they will say!' said Edward James, as he and Mr Manders swept, and dusted, and made up the bed.

'Why, they'll look at me, and say, "Good to see you again, old chap!" ' said Mr Manders. 'And then they'll look at you, and say, "What a big bear he is for his age!" '

'And then,' said Mr Manders, as he and Edward James made their way down the stairs for lunch, 'we'll take them exploring in the wood. We'll introduce them to Florence, and we'll take their photograph, posing by the begonia beds.'

Edward James felt that he couldn't wait until the visitors arrived, and he went to bed early so that the morning would come more quickly.

Early next morning, there came a loud rat-tat-tat at the door. Mr Manders hurried to open it, and in strode Bickers and Wilkins. They were the biggest bears that Edward James had ever seen. They wore huge boots, and carried picks and great coils of rope. 'We've been climbing moun-

47

tains!' they said, in loud, deep voices.

They shook Mr Manders's hand, and said, 'Good to see you, old chap!'

And, just as Mr Manders had said they would, they patted Edward James on the head, and said, 'What a big bear he is for his age!' Then Bickers lifted him up, tossed him to the ceiling, and caught him in his huge paws. 'That's what small bears like!' he said.

Wilkins sat down on Mr Manders's armchair, took Edward James on his knee, and jogged him up and down. 'This is what small bears like!' he said.

But Edward James liked neither of these things; being tossed to the ceiling made him dizzy, and being jogged up and down made him feel sick.

For the rest of the day Bickers and Wilkins stayed in the house, and talked about the adventures they had had while climbing mountains. They were not at all interested in the begonia beds, and they scarcely listened when Mr Manders told them about visiting the mysterious island in the pond. They were a little more interested in the boat, but when Mr Manders and Edward James took them over the field to look at it, they just said, 'Ah, yes – nice little craft!' Then they went back to the house, where they ate great quantities of scrambled eggs and toast.

When they had eaten, they threw Edward James up to the ceiling and jogged him on their knees again. In the evening they sang, and their deep, rumbling voices seemed to fill the whole house.

The next morning, Mr Manders and Edward James took Bickers and Wilkins down to the summer house, to meet Florence. Bickers and Wilkins were most polite, and took Florence's little paw in their own, and said, 'Pleased to meet you, M'am.' But Florence merely sniffed, and took her paw back. 'Shy little thing!' said Wilkins, as they made their way back to the garden; but

Edward James knew that Florence hadn't really liked the visitors very much.

When they reached the begonia bed, Mr Manders wanted Bickers and Wilkins to pose for a photograph, but Bickers said that they only posed for photographs when they were doing something brave or exciting.

In the afternoon, Mr Manders and Edward James took Bickers and Wilkins to the woods to explore. 'I hope that something exciting happens,' said Mr Manders, as he and Edward James walked behind the two big bears. 'It's very difficult when you have visitors who are used to exciting things happening all the time.'

'Perhaps they'll meet the orange cat,' said Edward James.

But Mr Manders just looked thoughtful, and said, 'I don't think they would find that very exciting.' Then he looked a little brighter, and said, 'But there *might* be a real tiger in the wood, Edward James. After all, we didn't explore *all* of it.'

They sat side by side, near the bush where they had first seen the cat, and watched as the two big bears strode off between the trees. 'What will they do if they see a tiger?' asked Edward James.

'Do?' said Mr Manders, 'Why they'll just say,

"Ah-ha!! A tiger!" and capture him, and bring him back with them.'

Edward James was thrilled at the idea of the visitors coming back with a tiger; but when the two bears returned, they were alone. And they just said, 'Jolly nice little wood you've got here!'

'Did you see a tiger by any chance?' asked Mr Manders. But Bickers and Wilkins merely laughed, and said, '*Tiger?* You won't find any tigers in *this* wood, old thing.'

In the evening, they sang songs again. 'Join in, old chap!' they said to Mr Manders. But when Mr Manders tried to join in he didn't always know the words, and when he did know the words, his voice was drowned by the loud voices of the two big bears. They sang about being lost in the jungle, about being tossed on the waves of the sea, and about climbing mountains.

Edward James thought the songs would never end; but at last they did, and Wilkins kindly took Edward James on his knees, and said, 'Care to be jogged up and down, little chap?'

'No, thank you,' said Edward James, and he scampered up to bed.

The next morning, Bickers and Wilkins collected their picks, took their coils of rope from the hook in the hall, and said their goodbyes. Mr

Manders and Edward James went with them as far as the gate at the edge of the field; then they stood and watched as Bickers and Wilkins strode off down the lane, still singing, and waving their huge paws.

Mr Manders was rather quiet for the rest of the day. In the evening he and Edward James went for a walk round the garden. Round and round they went, in silence, until at last Mr Manders sighed deeply, and said, 'They are such large friends, Edward James, and they've done such exciting things.'

'You've done exciting things too,' said Edward James. 'You've been up in a balloon, you've built a boat, and you've visited the mysterious island on the pond.'

'But I never got a chance to tell them,' said Mr Manders. 'You see, Edward James, when you have visitors it should be like a game – they tell you all about the exciting things that they've done, and then it's your turn to tell them about the exciting things that *you* have done. Somehow, when you've done exciting things, you want to talk about them.'

'Write them a letter!' suggested Edward James. He felt a little angry with Bickers and Wilkins, for not letting Mr Manders have his turn. 'Write them a letter and tell them all about everything.'

Mr Manders was very pleased with this idea,

and he went into the house at once, and got out his pen and his writing pad. Edward James sat in the armchair, and listened as Mr Manders read his letter aloud. 'Dear Bickers and Wilkins, I don't think I remembered to tell you how Edward James and I went up in a balloon. It was a very exciting event. It began one bright and windy morning, when Edward James found the balloon in the attic. Off we went, our hearts and our courage high. . . .' It was a wonderful letter, but Edward James heard no more of it, for he had fallen asleep.

In the summer house, Florence was writing to her great-aunt Tomkins. She described the two bears, and how they had tramped all over the garden and the field. 'Mr Manders admires them, I think; but as for myself, I am not fond of *very* large bears. Mr Manders, who is in fact a rather shy and quiet bear, is quite big enough for me.'

Edward James leaves Home

Mr Manders made wonderful toast and beautiful birthday cakes, but his porridge was full of lumps. He made it every Tuesday morning, and Edward James hated it. 'Lumpy, bumpy porridge!' he said.

'Eat your breakfast,' said Mr Manders.

Edward James hit his porridge with his spoon. Lumps and bumps flew from the bowl. Some landed on the tablecloth, and one landed on Mr Manders's nose. He was rather annoyed. 'Eat your breakfast,' he said, once more.

'No!' shouted Edward James. 'I hate lumpy porridge, and I'm going to run away from home!' Before Mr Manders could say anything, Edward James jumped down from his chair, and ran out into the garden and through the gap in the fence.

Mr Manders watched him go from the kitchen window. Then he picked up the bowl of porridge and put it on the stove, to keep warm. 'He'll soon come back,' he said, and he went outside to weed the begonia beds.

But Edward James marched right through the field, down the lane, and into the deep, dark wood. At first he sang a song to himself as he went, but when he reached the middle of the wood he stopped and looked around. He had reached the bush where he and Mr Manders had seen the orange cat, and had thought it was a tiger. Now, two green eyes looked at Edward James from amongst the leaves. Suppose this time it really *is* a tiger? he thought.

Edward James wished that Mr Manders was with him, then he could say, carelessly, 'It's only an orange cat!'

And Mr Manders would say, 'Of course it is!'

But there was no Mr Manders; only the tall, dark trees, and the bush with the two green, winking eyes. As Edward James sat and stared, the orange cat came strolling from the bush. When he saw Edward James, he sat down in front of him, lifted a paw, and tickled him under the chin. Edward James felt a little better at this, for tigers don't usually tickle one under the chin.

'Simpson,' said the cat, lying down and introducing himself. 'And what is a small bear doing alone in the wood?'

'I've run away from home,' said Edward James.

He felt quite proud of himself, and hoped that Simpson would ask how he had got to the middle of the wood, all by himself. But Simpson only yawned, and said, 'Small creatures usually run away from home. But they always run back again.'

'*I* won't run back!' said Edward James.

'Of course not,' said Simpson. 'Neither did I. Shall I tell you,' he said, making himself a little

more comfortable, 'how I ran away from home?'

'Yes!' said Edward James. He was very pleased. He had only been away from home for an hour or so, and already he had made a friend, and was going to be told an exciting story. He almost wished that he *was* going home, then he could tell Mr Manders all about it.

'I'll begin,' said Simpson. And, sitting up quite straight, he said, in a very loud voice, 'HOW I RAN AWAY FROM HOME, AND MADE A NEW LIFE, ALONE IN THE WOOD!'

The loudness of Simpson's voice startled Edward James. 'I beg your pardon,' said Simpson, 'but I had to shout because, you see, if my story were in a book that would be the title, in big, bold letters. But I can't write a book,' he added, settling down again. 'Mainly because I haven't got a pencil; have you got a pencil at home?'

'Lots,' said Edward James, thinking of the dresser drawer in the kitchen, which was full of pencils; some coloured, some chewed at the end (when Mr Manders had trouble writing a letter), and some with little india rubbers on the end.

'What a lucky little bear you are!' said Simpson. 'But, to go on with my tale: I was born one of a litter of six. Some of us were striped, but I was the only orange one. "Simpson, my little orange dumpling," my mother used to call me.

Are you listening?'

'Yes,' said Edward James, wondering when the exciting bit of the story would start.

'I had a wonderful kittenhood,' said Simpson. 'Rumble-tumble over the hay we went ... rumbley-tumbley over the green grass. . . .'

His voice grew softer and slower as he spoke, until it stopped altogether, and he seemed to fall asleep. Edward James was disappointed. Mr Manders told very good stories, and he always started with an exciting bit. But all that Simpson would say, when Edward James gave him a little shake, was 'Rumbley-tumbley over the hay. . . .' And then he went to sleep again.

Edward James sighed. He was beginning to feel rather lonely. And the wood, as he sat and listened, seemed full of strange sounds. It wasn't at all like sitting in the garden with Mr Manders, listening to the sounds that he knew: the babble of the stream, the hum of the bees in the flowers, and the sound of Florence singing in the summer house as she made a treacle tart for tea.

He sat for a long time, and at last Simpson awoke. 'Where was I?' he asked. 'Ah, yes ... rumbley-tumbley over the grass—'

'You've said that bit,' interrupted Edward James. 'What happened next?'

'Not a lot,' said Simpson. 'I grew into a big cat, and ran away to live in the wood. It's a nice, quiet life, you know. One sits in one's bush. One prowls about a bit, and sleeps a bit.'

'Have you got a little bed, with a patchwork quilt?' asked Edward James, thinking of his own little bedroom.

'Patchwork quilt?' said Simpson. 'No, I can't say that I have. One sleeps on a few leaves. It gets a bit damp in the morning, and one's paws get a bit wet.'

'Wet paws?' said Edward James, thinking of how careful Mr Manders was that neither he nor Edward James got wet paws. 'Don't you get a cold in the head?'

'All the time,' said Simpson, 'but one puts up with it.' And he sneezed three times and shook his head.

'You need a hot lemon drink,' said Edward James, thinking of how Mr Manders always made him a glass of hot lemon whenever he had a cold in the head.

'Hot lemon?' said Simpson. 'By George, do you have hot lemon? Why, I think you could search this wood from beginning to end, and not find one lemon, either hot *or* cold.'

Then slowly his head sank down until it lay on his neatly folded paws, and he went to sleep once more. Edward James sat and watched him. 'Simpson,' he said, from time to time.

But Simpson only murmured, 'Rumble-tumble,' or, 'Hot lemon,' in his sleep.

Little by little, the wood began to grow dark, and Edward James began to feel very hungry. At last Simpson woke up again, and began to scratch his left ear. 'I'm hungry,' said Edward James. 'What do you have for tea?'

'Tea?' said Simpson. 'Well, you might find a few berries here and there, you know. But be careful not to eat poisonous ones!'

Edward James thought about how Mr Manders would be making toast for tea; how he would be sitting close by the stove, with the little door open, holding the thick slices of bread to the glowing coals. His tummy began to rumble. 'Do you have toast for tea?' he said.

'Toast?' said Simpson. 'Of course I don't have toast. Mainly because I don't have a toasting fork. Have you got a toasting fork?'

'Yes,' said Edward James, and a lump came into his throat, as he thought of the bright, brass toasting fork hanging from its nail in the kitchen.

'What a lucky little bear you are!' said Simpson. 'Pencils! Patchwork quilts! Hot lemons and toasting forks! What a wonderful life!'

'Yes, it is!' said Edward James, and he jumped to his feet.

'Thank you for the story,' he said. 'It was very interesting, but I must go home now!' And he turned and ran, and didn't stop until he reached the field and could see, in the distance, the house with the kitchen door standing open to welcome him, and Mr Manders himself coming down the garden path.

'There you are, Edward James,' he said. 'I've been looking everywhere for you!'

'Oh, Mr Manders!' said Edward James. 'I'm so glad to be home!'

In the wood, Simpson got up and stretched himself, and began to make his way between the trees. As he went, the setting sun shone on the little silver medal he wore round his neck. On the medal were these words: 'My name is Simpson, and I live at Davenport farm.'

'Little bears shouldn't be encouraged to run away from home,' said Simpson with a smile, and he padded softly through the farmyard and into the house, for his tea.

Thunder and Lightning

One hot and sultry day, the sky grew very dark. Great black clouds rolled in over the field, the pond and the garden. Mr Manders and Edward James went outside, to see what was happening. They found everything very still and quiet. Not one bird sang in the tree, and the fieldmice, who played together in the long grass, had all scuttled back to their homes. It was as if the whole garden was holding its breath. 'Something is going to happen,' said Mr Manders.

'What?' asked Edward James.

'I'm not sure,' said Mr Manders, and he set off down the path, to look at the field and the pond. Edward James trotted close behind.

When they reached the field, not a blade of

grass was stirring and the pond lay as still as a pond made of glass. Above their heads was just one small patch of blue sky; and then, quite suddenly, it vanished. The black clouds came together, the thunder rumbled and the lightning flashed. Huge drops of rain began to fall. They hit Edward James on the nose, and bounced off again – Edward James quite liked it, but Mr Manders took hold of his paw, and hurried him back through the gap in the fence.

'Don't stand under a tree!' he said, as they went. 'Don't touch metal! Don't put up an umbrella!'

'What?' said Edward James, who hadn't thought of doing any of these things.

'Don't stand under a brolly!' gabbled Mr Manders. 'Don't touch a tree!' Then they reached the house, ran into the kitchen, and closed the door with a slam.

They were only just in time, for as soon as they closed the door there was a loud clap of thunder and a flash of lightning that lit up the kitchen. It made everything stand out very clearly – the pattern of roses on the carpet, the kitchen dresser standing against the wall, and the portrait of Mr Manders's ancestor, Darcy Manders the bold balloonist. Everything, for that one moment, was as clear as day. Even the scents and smells were clearer; the scent of roses in the garden and

63

the faint smell of the toast they had had for tea. But there was a new smell in the room, too. It was the smell of someone who was afraid. Edward James's nose traced the smell to Mr Manders, sitting stiff and upright in his big armchair. The smell made a funny feeling in the bottom of Edward James's tummy, and he scuttled under the kitchen table, where it was safe and dark.

'What are you doing there, silly little bear?' said Mr Manders.

Then, Crack! went the thunder, the lightning flashed, and Mr Manders crawled quickly across the floor, and sat halfway under the table with the tablecloth draped over his head. 'I just came to see if you were all right,' he said.

He looked rather funny with the bobbles of the tablecloth hanging over his nose. Edward James began to laugh. 'That's the thing to do!' said Mr Manders. 'One must just laugh at these storms.' He said, 'Ha-ha!' in a loud voice; but Edward James could tell that he didn't really mean it.

'The thing to do,' said Mr Manders, 'at a time like this, is to comfort those who are perhaps feeling a little uneasy.' And he patted Edward James's head with a quivering paw. 'A friendly word, a comforting touch: that's what is needed,' he said.

Edward James came out from beneath the table, and went to look through the window. The funny feeling in his tummy had gone, and he wanted to see what was happening in the garden. It was very dark outside, and the bushes seemed to have grown bigger and denser. Rain bounced on the ground and there, right at the end of the path, was the lighted window of the summer house, with the figure of Florence, standing and waving her arms.

'Mr Manders,' said Edward James. 'I think that Florence wants a friendly word and a comforting touch.'

'What?' said Mr Manders. He came slowly from beneath the table, and stood at Edward James's side. 'I'm afraid that you're right,' he said. 'She is beside herself with fear. We must go to her at once! The thing to do,' he said, as they went down the hall, 'is to say to yourself, "I am not afraid!" '

They opened the door, and stepped out on to the path. But they had scarcely taken a dozen steps, when the thunder gave the loudest crack of all and the lightning flashed in the sky. It seemed to strike the path just in front of them and, with a yelp of fright, they both turned and ran back to the house as quickly as they could. Edward James reached the door first and, without waiting for Mr Manders, slammed it closed. Mr Manders reached the door and tried to turn the knob, but it just slipped round and round in his wet paws. 'Edward James!' he shouted. 'Open the door!'

In the hall, Edward James looked at the door knob turning this way and that. 'Mr Manders!' he shouted, and took hold of the knob. But as he tried to turn it one way, Mr Manders tried to turn it the other; and so they stood, shouting, 'Edward James!' and, 'Mr Manders!' while the thunder rolled about in the sky and the flashes of lightning went Crack! Crack! Crack! all over the garden.

At last they both turned the knob the same way. The door opened, and Mr Manders staggered into the hall. He was very wet, and rainwater dripped in a little pool around him. For a few moments he stood in this little pool and gazed at Edward James. 'You might have heard me calling,' he said, at last. 'But I was only calling in case you were frightened.'

'*I* wasn't frightened,' said Edward James. 'I was calling in case *you* were frightened.'

'*I* wasn't frightened,' said Mr Manders.

Together they went back to the kitchen and looked down the path, to where Florence stood waving her arms at each clap of thunder and flash of lightning. She really did look very frightened indeed. 'We must go to her, no matter what happens,' said Mr Manders.

He marched out of the house, with Edward James marching behind him. Down the path they went, leaving the door open behind them. 'Just in case some small creature wishes to find shelter,' said Mr Manders.

Edward James took hold of Mr Manders's paw as they went along, and tried to imagine lots of small, wet furry creatures, all sheltering in the kitchen. There they would be when he and Mr Manders returned, he thought, all sitting in a row, drying their fur before the stove. 'Have you come in from the storm?' he would say, in a kind voice, 'Me and Mr Manders have been out in it, to rescue Florence, you know.' And he would hum a little tune, to show that he hadn't been frightened at all.

Then Clap! went the thunder, and Crack! went the lightning. Mr Manders and Edward James stood still, and thought of the safe, warm kitchen behind them. Then Mr Manders made a sort of gulping noise and said, in a voice not quite like his own, 'The thing to do, Edward James, is not to look back.'

'Onward!' he cried, staggering forwards and pulling Edward James along with him. 'One must think of one's brave ancestors! One must ask oneself, what would Darcy Manders have done?'

'What would he do?' squeaked Edward James.

'He would cry "Ha-ha!" ' said Mr Manders.

'Ha-ha!' cried Edward James – and with that they stumbled into the summer house.

Florence turned from the window as they entered. 'Mr Manders,' she said. 'You are making a pool of rainwater on my floor.'

'But we have come to rescue you!' said Mr Manders.

'I don't need rescuing,' said Florence, firmly. 'I quite like a storm.' She turned back to the window and waved her arms. 'Ha-ha!' she cried as the thunder clouds rumbled, and the lightning lit up the garden once more.

'Oh,' said Mr Manders. 'I see.'

As he spoke, the black clouds suddenly rolled away, the sky became blue once more and the whole garden stood before them, all green and wet, and full of fresh delightful smells.

Paw in paw, Mr Manders and Edward James went splashing back down the path. They walked slowly, and looked around them as they went. 'The thing is,' said Mr Manders, as they reached the kitchen door, 'that one has been *brave*. That's the thing to remember, Edward James. It doesn't matter that Florence didn't need us. We were brave, and said, "Ha-ha!" in the teeth of the storm.'

They went then into the kitchen, and found the floor full of tiny, muddy paw marks, where small frightened creatures had scampered in for shelter (though there were no small creatures now to be seen). 'Mr Manders and I have been to rescue Florence,' said Edward James, in case just one remained, hiding behind the dresser. 'We weren't at all afraid!'

And then, because being brave can make you feel very hungry, he and Mr Manders had tea again: toast, and boiled eggs, and cherry cake, and pie.

A Visit from a Tiger

One bright and sunny morning, Simpson decided that he would pay Edward James and Mr Manders a visit. Edward James saw him from the window of the tree house as he came weaving his way through the long grass of the field, and scrambled down the tree, to tell Mr Manders. But as he came down, he was surprised to see Florence making her way up; quickly, from branch to branch she went, as nimble as a squirrel. When she reached the tree house, she went inside and closed the door with a slam. 'There's a tiger in the field!' Edward James heard her shout.

'It isn't a tiger,' said Edward James. 'It's a cat.'

'Indeed!' said Florence.

Mr Manders came from the house, climbed the tree and knocked on the door. 'It's Edward James's friend,' he said, in a soothing voice. 'He's called Simpson.'

'Tigers always give themselves nice names,' said Florence, from behind the door. 'But no matter what they call themselves, they are still tigers.' And nothing that Mr Manders, or Edward James could say would convince her that Simpson was just a large and friendly cat.

Mr Manders and Edward James hurried through the gap in the fence to greet Simpson, and to explain the matter to him. Simpson said that he would stay quietly in the field, until the problem with Florence was settled, and he stretched out beneath the hedge and went to sleep. Mr Manders and Edward James went back to the garden.

Florence was standing by the open tree house door. 'Mr Manders,' she said. 'Now that the tiger is asleep, would you bring up my little workbox, please?'

So Mr Manders went to the summer house, found the little workbox, and carried it up the tree. 'Thank you, Mr Manders,' said Florence, opening the box and disclosing the reels of cotton, the tape measure, the scissors, and the shining needles. 'Now bring up my little wicker trunk,' she said.

Mr Manders and Edward James went to the summer house and dragged the little wicker trunk along the garden path. Then Mr Manders tied a rope to the handle of the trunk, threw the end of the rope over a stout branch, and hauled the trunk up into the tree. Florence opened the trunk and began to take out lengths of brightly patterned cotton. 'Thank you, Mr Manders,' she said. 'If I am forced to live up here on account of a tiger, then I shall make myself some new curtains.'

'Live up there?' said Mr Manders. 'But he isn't a tiger, and he is only here on a short visit.'

'Tigers never pay short visits,' said Florence,

firmly. 'They always stay for a long time.' She closed the door of the tree house, and Mr Manders and Edward James heard the snick-snick of her scissors, as she began to cut out the curtains.

Mr Manders and Edward James hurried to the field, where Simpson lay beneath the hedge. He was still asleep, and he looked comfortable and contented. Mr Manders and Edward James went back to the kitchen, and Mr Manders began to make some fish paste sandwiches. 'I do like to make a guest feel welcome,' he said, and he covered the plate with a little white cloth, in readiness for when Simpson awoke. Then he and Edward James went back to the garden and looked up into the branches of the tree.

Florence was standing by the tree house door. 'Mr Manders,' she said, 'would you be kind enough to bring up my sewing machine? I can sew much faster with a sewing machine.'

Mr Manders and Edward James went to the summer house, and pushed Florence's sewing machine up the path. It had a big wheel, and a treadle made of iron, and it was very heavy. 'Heave!' cried Mr Manders and Edward James as they pulled on the rope to haul the machine into the tree. Slowly, it disappeared into the leaves, and they heard Florence trundle it into the tree house. Soon after, they heard the whirr-whirr sound of the machine, as Florence began to make the new curtains.

Mr Manders and Edward James went back to the kitchen. They were very hungry after hauling the machine up into the tree, so they ate one or two of the sandwiches.

'Life has its problems,' said Mr Manders, as he and Edward James ate. 'One expects that, of course. And one wouldn't mind if they came one at a time.'

For a while they sat and thought sadly of all their problems. Edward James wondered if Florence would ever come out of his tree house, and Mr Manders wondered how he could make her believe that Simpson was a cat. Then they both wondered if Simpson's feelings were hurt by being left alone in the field. Mr Manders took the plate of sandwiches, and he and Edward James hurried back to where Simpson lay by the hedge.

They found Simpson awake, and smoothing his whiskers. 'How-de-do!' he said. He seemed pleased to see them and, after staying with him for a little while, Mr Manders and Edward James left him sitting with a fish paste sandwich held delicately in his paw. 'But it's no way to treat a guest!' said Mr Manders, as they trotted back up the garden path, to the tree.

When they got there, they found that the whirring of the machine had stopped, and that Florence was standing by the tree house door. 'It's time for lunch, Mr Manders,' she said. 'Would you bring up my tea set, a loaf of bread, a pot of jam, and a pat of butter; also the framed photograph of my great-aunt Tomkins.'

Mr Manders sighed, went to the summer house, put all these things in a basket, and carried them up the tree. Edward James climbed up behind him. His special place looked very different. It's Florence's tree house now, he thought, as he watched her set out the tea cups, and the photograph.

'The thing to do, Edward James,' said Mr Manders, when they climbed back down the tree, 'is to bring Simpson into the garden – then Florence can hear us talking happily about the weather, and all the things that one talks to a visitor about. After all,' he added, 'one doesn't talk to a tiger about the weather.'

They began to make their way back to the gap in the fence. (As they went, Edward James wondered what one *would* talk to a tiger about – but Mr Manders said that was quite another problem.)

Simpson was dozing by the empty plate. When he awoke, he agreed at once to come to the garden. But even though he, Edward James and Mr Manders sat for quite a long time, chatting beneath the tree, the tree house door didn't open, and Florence didn't come out.

At last, Simpson said, 'Give her my respects, and tell her *I* say I am not a tiger.'

Mr Manders climbed the tree, and opened the door. 'He says he's not a tiger,' he said.

'They all say that,' said Florence firmly.

There was nothing more to be said, and nothing to be done, thought Mr Manders; and he turned to go. But Florence reached out a paw and touched him gently on the arm. 'I would like very much for you and Edward James to spend the rest of the day with me,' she said.

Mr Manders looked at her. She was sitting on Edward James's cushions, with the neat pile of new curtains by her side. 'I find living in a tree house rather lonely,' she said.

Mr Manders was surprised. 'But you don't mind living alone in the summer house,' he said.

'Some places you aren't lonely in, even when you are on your own – and some you are,' said Florence, firmly.

So there was nothing to be done but for Edward James and Mr Manders to climb the tree, and for the three of them to sit crowded together in the tree house. They sat knee to knee, and almost nose to nose – for, after all, the tree house had been made just for one small bear, and the sewing machine itself took up a great deal of room. Simpson lay beneath the tree and, from time to time Mr Manders and Edward James shouted some remark down to him, and Simpson shouted back.

But it was not at all a satisfactory state of things and, to make matters worse, just before tea a strong wind began to blow. The tree house began to rock and the sewing machine began to trundle its way over the floor, going first one way and then the other.

Edward James sat and wondered if he could have the summer house as his special place, and if he would like it as much as the tree house. Mr Manders sat and thought about how his problems had grown – and of how this latest problem was the strangest of all – the problem of whether or not he would be run over by a sewing machine.

At the foot of the tree, Simpson sat and thought that it was time that he went home. But he was a polite cat, and he didn't like leaving without saying goodbye. (And it seemed ill-mannered merely to shout 'Goodbye!' up into a tree.) So he climbed the trunk and put his head round the door.

At this, Florence leapt to her feet, took hold of the curtains, and began to flap them furiously in his face. Mr Manders jumped up to stop her, but the machine trundled by and trapped him in a corner. Edward James jumped up to help Mr Manders, but tripped over the cushions and turned a somersault.

Simpson looked at them all in amazement. 'Thank you for the fish paste sandwiches,' he said. Then he carefully closed the door and went back down the tree.

Mr Manders and Edward James gazed through the window, and watched him pad over the garden, through the gap in the fence, and out across the field. 'Goodbye, Simpson. Goodbye!' they called. They were sorry to see him go, for they had had little of his company, and he seemed a gentle and interesting creature. But when they turned back to Florence they found her calmly folding the curtains, with a look of great satisfaction on her face. '*That's* the way to treat tigers,' she said, firmly. 'And now, Mr Manders, I would like to go home.'

The Poem

One morning, Mr Manders woke up with the feeling that he would like to write a poem. He had never had the feeling before, and he hurried to wake the little bear to tell him all about it. 'It's a very special feeling,' he said, 'and bears don't often get it. The thing to do is to write the poem as quickly as you can, before the feeling goes.'

He hurried down the stairs, with Edward James behind him, and took his pencil and his writing pad from the dresser drawer. Then he sat down in the armchair, and waited for the poem to begin.

'What is the poem about?' asked Edward James, after some time had passed and Mr Manders had neither spoken nor written anything.

'Well, that's the puzzling thing about poetry,' said Mr Manders. 'Sometimes you don't know right away what it will be about – it just sort of happens.

'And it must rhyme,' he added. Then he said, very quickly:

'I sit in a chair,
And stare at a bear,
Who is waiting there,
For me to write a POEM.'

Edward James liked this little poem so much that he wanted Mr Manders to say it again. But Mr Manders said that a poem should be about something important, not just about a bear sitting in a chair, staring at another bear. He ate his breakfast as quickly as he could, put on his jacket, and went out across the garden and through the gap in the fence.

When he reached the middle of the field, he flung up his paw in the air, and shouted aloud:

'Oh, wondrous field!
Oh, field divine!
How glad I am that you are mine.
How I wish to share your joys,
With all the little girls and boys.'

He was very pleased with his poem, and said it again as he walked over the grass. But then he thought that he didn't know any girls and boys –

and even if he did, he wasn't at all sure that he would like them to be in his field. And although he had never written a poem before, he somehow knew that what a poem said must be the truth. 'One just can't put a lie in a poem,' he said to himself.

He reached the stream, sat down on the bank, and flung up his paw once more:

'Oh, wondrous and delightful stream!

Sometimes I think you are a dream!'

But that wasn't true either. He knew that his stream wasn't a dream; it was babbling away at his feet, and it was real.

Edward James and Florence watched all this from the gap in the fence. They watched as Mr Manders got slowly to his feet and went to stand beneath the tree in the garden. They watched as he flung up a paw and cried, 'Oh, wondrous tree!'

Then they watched as he stood over his flowerbeds, and cried:

'Oh, begonias red, and all a-bloom!

How oft you cheer my hours of gloom!'

Edward James and Florence looked at one another. 'Hours of *gloom*?' said Florence. Then they hurried on, for Mr Manders was making his way back to the field. But this time, instead of flinging up a paw, he clasped both paws behind his back and, staring down at his feet, he marched about, muttering to himself:

'As I go wandering over the grass,
I think of what might come to pass.
I think of battles long ago,
Of tales of misery and woe!'

'Misery and woe?' said Edward James. 'He doesn't think about that at all!'

For the rest of the morning Edward James and Florence followed Mr Manders round the field and garden, as he tried to make up his poem. Sometimes he flung up a paw, and cried, 'Oh wondrous hedge!' And sometimes he clasped his paws behind his back and looked at the ground and muttered, 'Oh, long and lonely little path!'

At last, when the clock struck twelve, Florence took him by the arm, marched him firmly into the kitchen and set a slice of pie before him, with a large helping of greens. But, instead of eating, Mr Manders merely stared at his plate and said:

'Oh charming little piece of pie,
Perhaps I'll eat you by and by.'

The afternoon was just the same as the morning. Mr Manders wandered about, from garden to field, and along the banks of the stream. Sometimes he said, 'Oh, wondrous!' And sometimes he said, 'Divine!' (But he no longer flung up a paw.)

When tea time came, Florence brought a treacle tart which she had baked, to cheer him up. But he merely looked at her and sighed, and said 'There's nothing that rhymes with Florence, but there's quite a lot that rhymes with Flo. There's "Go", and "So" and "No", and "Oh".'

'Indeed!' said Florence. 'Mr Manders, you are getting rather silly!' And she marched off down the path to the summer house and firmly closed the door. Mr Manders saw this from the window, and he jumped to his feet:

'Oh, she has firmly closed the door!' (he cried)

'And she will open it never more!'

At this, Edward James began to laugh. 'Of course she will!' he said.

Mr Manders sat down again in his chair. 'I know it,' he said sadly. 'It's just that no matter how hard I try, I just can't write a poem about something important, like the field, or a tree, or Florence returning never more.'

'It doesn't matter,' said Edward James.

'I tried and I tried,' said Mr Manders. 'But nothing I thought of was right, or true.'

'Try again,' said Edward James. 'Perhaps the poem will come this time.'

So Mr Manders sat for a time, and at last he

sighed, and said:

> 'I sit in a chair,
> And stare at a bear
> Who is waiting there
> For me to write a poem.'

There was a long silence after this. Then, 'I *like* it!' said Edward James.

A. Mole

Early one morning, when Mr Manders went out into the garden, he found a small black hill right in the middle of his lawn. He was rather annoyed, but he was also rather puzzled. Clearly, the little hill had been made by someone; for little hills don't make themselves, suddenly, in the night.

Mr Manders walked round the little hill and gazed at it; and the more he gazed, the more he felt certain that some small creature had made it for their home. Mr Manders smiled to think of the creature, digging away in the night, and making what it no doubt thought was a grand tower; for if one lay full length on the lawn, and half-closed one's eyes, the hill looked like the tower of a small castle. 'I might plant a few begonias around it,' said Mr Manders to himself. 'And then it will look a bit like another flowerbed.'

He went back into the kitchen and, after breakfast, he and Edward James went out to sail the boat across the pond. The little hill was quite forgotten until the next morning, when Mr Manders found another, bigger hill. 'I'm afraid that whatever this creature is, it is getting into the habit of making these hills,' Mr Manders told Edward James. 'It must be told to stop it at once!'

For the rest of the day they sat by the lawn, and kept a watch for the small creature, but there was no one to be seen. When evening came Mr Manders wrote a short letter, and propped it by one of the little hills. 'To whom it may concern,' it said, 'I don't mind you making your home on my lawn; you are very welcome. But please do not make any more hills. Yours respectfully, Mr Manders.'

The next morning he was surprised to find a letter addressed to him, lying on the lawn, and all wet with dew. 'Dear Sir,' it said, in large wobbling letters (for the dew had made the ink run a little). 'Thank you for your respected letter of the 5th. And for your kind invitation as to your green and wormy lawn. But might we respectfully point out that a body must have a back door as well as a front door. It says so in the regulations. Signed, A. Mole.'

A. Mole? thought Mr Manders. Regulations? Then he thought that he himself had a back door as well as a front door. 'And there's no reason I can think of, Edward James,' he said 'as to why A. Mole, whoever he is, shouldn't have the same number of doors.'

But the next morning he found another three hills on his lawn. They were rather untidily made, and looked as though they might fall down at any moment. This was too much, thought Mr Manders, and he wrote another letter – this time with a rather stern tone. 'Dear A. Mole. Kindly desist from making hills on my lawn. Yours respectfully, Mr Manders.'

The next morning there was yet another hill to be seen. Mr Manders gazed at his lawn, and thought of all the time he had spent sowing grass seed, cutting the grass when it grew, and rolling the lawn with the heavy roller so that it would be smooth and flat. He decided that he would stay up all night, and catch who ever was making the hills, and speak to him very firmly. When evening fell, he wrapped himself in his patchwork quilt, and sat down on the front doorstep.

The hours passed very slowly. But, at two in the morning, Mr Manders saw A. Mole come from one of the small black hills: first his two pink paws, like little hands; and then his long nose, on which was perched a pair of round spectacles; and then the rest of his body.

Carefully gathering his quilt about him, Mr Manders stepped over the lawn. 'Good evening!' he said, startling A. Mole. 'About these hills,' he went on, in a gentler voice – for he was sorry that he had made the little animal jump – 'I really can't put up with any more of them, you know.'

A. Mole said nothing to this, but merely took off his spectacles and carefully polished them with his handkerchief. Then he put them back on his nose, and gazed at Mr Manders.

'They will have to go,' said Mr Manders. 'That is, some of them will have to go . . . well, one or two of them.' He stopped, at a loss as to how to go on; for A. Mole still said nothing but just gazed at each of his hills in turn.

'I can understand a front door and a back door,' said Mr Manders, 'but surely you don't need so *many* doors.'

'It's like this,' said A. Mole, moving a little closer to Mr Manders, and speaking in a confiding kind of way. 'I comes up here (and he pointed to one of the hills) and *there's* a view! The view of your begonia beds. Then I come up *there* (and he pointed to another hill) and there's another view!

Then I comes up here, and here's another view! And each one as pretty as the last, if not prettier. So I says to myself, why should a body limit himself to one view, or even three views, when he could have a new one every day?'

And try as he might, Mr Manders could think of no reason why anybody should. 'I see,' he said. 'Good night, and sleep well.' And he plodded back over the lawn, trailing the patchwork quilt behind him.

During the following days he found more and more hills on what had once been his lawn. Some were quite neat, as though they had been patted down smooth by A. Mole's pink paws – but others were flung up, as though the little creature had hardly been able to contain his excitement. Sometimes Mr Manders squatted down beside them, and tried to see what A. Mole had seen when he had come burrowing up through the damp warm earth. 'It's a good idea, to try to see the other fellow's view,' he said to Edward James, trying to make the best of things. But the thought came to him that his own view had been completely spoiled, the view he had had of his smooth green lawn; for it now looked not like a lawn at all, but like a new and strange little country, full of small, black mountains.

He tried to keep a count of the hills, but at the end of the week he gave up, for there were far too many, and the lawn now looked like a battlefield. Mr Manders decided that he must make a new lawn – but where? He lay awake at night, and thought about the problem.

As he lay, he became aware of the sound of scrabbling paws. Going to his bedroom window and looking out, he saw A. Mole leaving by one of his many doors, carrying a small shabby suitcase tied up with string. The moonlight shone on his spectacles, and Mr Manders watched as he wandered about the garden, until at last he came to the gap in the fence, and disappeared from sight.

The next morning, when Mr Manders went into the garden, he found a very damp letter propped against one of the hills. 'Dear Sir,' it said, 'I am leaving, as one view is getting to look very like another. When life gets like that, it is time to move on. Yours respectfully, A. Mole.'

Mr Manders read this letter twice, then he put it into his jacket pocket and went to get the roller from the shed, to repair his ruined lawn. Edward James came to help him, and together they pushed the heavy roller back and forth until the ground was smooth and flat once more.

At the end of the tiring day they went for a peaceful stroll round the field. Mr Manders walked slowly, for his paws were heavy. But Edward James scampered along until, with a cry of alarm, he tripped over a little hill. Mr Manders bent to look at it. It was the work of A. Mole, he knew that at once; for the earth was flung up with abandon, as though by the paws of an excited little animal, eager to see what lay before him.

Mr Manders smiled, and gazed round the field. Then he took hold of Edward James's paw, and together they began to make their way back to the house. 'I wonder what he thinks of the view,' said Mr Manders, as they went.

New Year's Eve

It was New Year's Eve – a special time for looking back over the old year and looking forward to the new. But it was hard to find a quiet place in which to think of these things.

Mr Manders and Edward James had had the best Christmas ever, and never had the little house by the stream been so full of visitors. Bickers and Wilkins had arrived, with their picks and coils of rope and presents. Poskitt, Florence's nephew, had come for a visit with Florence's great-aunt Tomkins.

Great-aunt Tomkins told wonderful ghost stories, Bickers and Wilkins told jokes and riddles, and everyone sang carols. Florence made a huge Christmas pudding, and mince pies, and

Mr Manders made a beautiful Christmas cake. Poskitt behaved himself fairly well (though he laughed so much at Wilkins's jokes that he gave himself hiccups). There was a lot of coming and going along the garden path, between the house and the summer house, and shouts of, 'Merry Christmas!' Holly wreaths were hung on doors. Everyone was full of happiness and laughter, there was a party every day, and the New Year's Eve party was the loudest and happiest of all.

But, quite suddenly, in the middle of all the noise, Mr Manders began to feel that he would like to go and sit quietly by himself for a while. So he opened the front door and trotted off over the garden, through the gap in the fence and out across the field.

The field seemed very big and dark, but above his head the stars were shining brightly – hundreds and thousands of stars, all twinkling and sparkling. It made Mr Manders dizzy to look at them, and he sat down with a bump.

As he sat, he heard the pitter-pat of Edward James's paws, as he came running over the field. Mr Manders turned and looked at him. He was wearing a little woolly cap that Florence had knitted for him, and he held a squeaker in his paw. 'Hello, Edward James,' said Mr Manders.

'Hello,' said Edward James. 'Why are you sitting alone in the field?'

'I don't quite know,' said Mr Manders, standing up and taking Edward James's paw. 'I wanted
to think about the old year and all the things we
did, but somehow it's got jumbled up in my
head.'

Together, they began to walk over the field.
'The whole year has just flown away,' said Mr
Manders. 'I wanted to remember it before we
started a new one.'

'You found an island,' said Edward James.

'Yes,' said Mr Manders, remembering the
strange island where he had been so lonely in the
far-away summer.

'And you made up a poem,' said Edward James.

'It wasn't a very good one,' said Mr Manders.

'But it *was* a poem,' said Edward James. 'And that's what matters.'

They went a little way in silence, over the crisp, frosty grass; then, 'I ran away from home,' said Edward James.

'But you came back again,' said Mr Manders. 'I'm glad about that.'

'So am I,' said Edward James.

'But now we have done all these things,' said Mr Manders, 'and next year it will be something new.'

'What new things?' said Edward James. 'I like doing the things we have done before – that's what I like best!'

'So do I,' said Mr Manders. 'But new things happen, whether we want them to or not.'

'Will they be nice things?' asked Edward James.

'I don't know until they happen,' said Mr Manders. '*Some* of them will be nice – but perhaps not all of them.'

They reached the end of the field, and turned to look back at the lighted windows of the house. They could see the shadow of Florence and Poskitt on the curtains, and could hear, faintly, the sound of Bickers's deep laugh.

'Shall we go back to the party?' asked Edward James.

'Yes . . .' said Mr Manders, absent-mindedly. He was thinking of the past year, and whether, if he could, he would do the things he had done all over again. 'Would I?' he asked himself, as he and Edward James began to make their way back over the field. He was surprised when he answered himself with a firm, 'No!

'I wouldn't do it again, Edward James,' he said. 'A new year is exciting. It's like opening a book you have never read before.'

Above their heads, the stars shone brighter than ever, the new year bells began to ring, and from the house there came the sound of squeakers being blown. Edward James blew his own squeaker, as loudly as he could.

'That's the thing to do, Edward James!' said Mr Manders. 'The new year has started, and it will be full of good, exciting things!'

'Will it?' said Edward James.

'Yes!' said Mr Manders. 'And whatever happens, good or bad, there will always be you and me.'

'And Florence too,' said Edward James.

'And Florence too,' said Mr Manders – for there she was, coming over the field to meet them. 'A Happy New Year!' they shouted, as they ran towards her, 'A very, very Happy New Year!'